Annie Stewart is a part-time researcher and writer. She lives near Bury St Edmunds in Suffolk and is currently working on more Wilf stories.

THE ADVENTURES OF WILF

Annie Stewart

Book Guild Publishing
Sussex, England

First published in Great Britain in 2010 by
The Book Guild Ltd
Pavilion View
19 New Road
Brighton, BN1 1UF

Paperback edition 2011

Typesetting in Century Schoolbook by
Keyboard Services, Luton, Bedfordshire

Printed in Great Britain by
CPI Antony Rowe

A catalogue record for this book is available from
The British Library

ISBN 978 1 84624 670 8

For PAW

CONTENTS

The Den
PRYVIT

1

WILF AND THE LOST CHRISTMAS BONE

Wilf was not his usual cheerful self. It was Christmas and his owners, The Hard-Ups, were feeling the 'credit crunch'. They had announced to their children, Felix and Melissa, that there would be no presents this year, but even worse, in Wilf's view, there would be no Christmas bone for him!

Wilf looked forward to his Christmas bone as it was always fatter and bigger and better than all the others he had throughout the year. He decided to hold crisis talks with his gang.

Let me introduce you to Wilf's gang: there was Best Friend William, the black Labrador; Best Girlfriend Maisie, the West Highland terrier; Mutt Next Door Joe; Pretty Polly Poodle and last, but not least, Posh Algie, the English Setter, who lived at the Big House and got lots of treats. Wilf himself is a scruffy Border terrier.

The gang met up at their den in the fields by the

river and tried to think what to do next. They were all very upset that Wilf was not going to get a Christmas bone but everyone's owners were saying the same thing. After much discussion it was decided that they should share their remaining bones and hide Wilf's last bone for after Christmas.

Christmas came and went and Wilf made the best of it by sulking and chasing the cats in the hope that the Hard-Ups would give in and buy him a bone but, as I am sure you can guess, they did not. Wilf and his gang had a New Year meeting at their riverside den and it was decided to start the hunt for Wilf's bone as they had all run out, even Algie – 'Sorry, old chap, my humans are saying things are so bad, they might even have to sell up.' This was very bad news as Algie's owners, Lord and Lady Hetherington-Smythe, of Montmorency Hall, usually had a plentiful supply of marrow bones.

The gang were very gloomy, particularly as Wilf could not remember where he had hidden his last bone. He knew it was in a safe place, but where? The hunt was on because the gang wanted to have a field sleepover with a midnight feast to cheer themselves up. Well, they searched high and low but could not find the bone anywhere. For two long days and nights they searched but found nothing, by which time everyone was really cross with Wilf, except Maisie, who always forgave him everything. The Hard-Ups were so angry with Wilf for digging up the entire

garden that he was grounded for a week. It was a disaster, until one day, between chasing the cats, sulking in his basket and generally driving Mrs Hard-Up mad, he remembered...

A new family had moved in up the road called the Well-Loadeds. They had three very noisy little boys called Tom, Dean and Harry and a very loud Jack Russell called Archie, who was always getting into trouble. One day Archie had got into Wilf's garden and a fight had started because Archie had found Wilf's precious last bone and was trying to steal it. Mrs Well-Loaded came round to say how sorry she was about Archie's behaviour to Mrs Hard-Up and, much to Wilf's disgust, they got quite friendly over chocolate cake and a cup of tea. This meant that Wilf had to put up with frequent noisy visits from Tom, Dean and Harry, who were now best mates with Felix and Melissa, as well as Archie, who further disgraced himself by chasing Wilf's cats and playing with his toys. Wilf knew that Archie had stolen his bone and hidden it in his garden; he had to get it back.

'Maisie,' Wilf said, 'you are the best digger, so you should get into Archie's garden after dark and try to get my bone back. I know he really likes you, so he will listen to what you have to say and you might be able to persuade him to do the right thing and return the bone.'

'I'll do my best, Wilfie,' promised Maisie.

Darkness fell and Maisie crept into Archie's garden

through a gap in the hedge. Archie was lying outside the back door nibbling on a bone.

'Hello, Maisie, how lovely to see you. Come and share some of my bone,' said Archie.

Maisie recognised Wilf's bone at once. 'Archie,' she cried, 'that is Wilf's Christmas bone and you had no right to take it! Wilf is very upset: he has dug up the whole garden looking for it and now Mr and Mrs Hard-Up have grounded him for a week.'

'Oh, Maisie,' said Archie, 'I'm so sorry, don't be cross, I never meant to upset you or Wilf or the others. Please let me make it up to you all.'

So what do you think Archie did? He shared all his Christmas bones with the gang as a peace offering. The Well-Loadeds were *not* feeling the credit crunch and Archie had bones galore!

Soon Wilf was back to his normal cheerful self, and Archie was sworn in as a member of Wilf's gang at a special ceremony held in the field, followed by a delicious bone buffet. Everyone was happy except the Hard-Ups, who could not understand where all the bones were coming from. However, when they realised that they were presents from their new friends, the Well-Loadeds, they were happy too. The 'credit crunch Christmas' had been a great success and taught everyone that sharing was great fun!

The Den
PRYVIT

2

WILF AND THE LAME DUCK

Spring had sprung in the little village of Montmorency St Peters, and Wilf and his gang were busy spring-cleaning their riverside den.

Wilf, along with Best Friend William, the black Labrador, Mutt Next Door Joe and Pretty Polly Poodle, in a very fetching red and white spotted apron, had been hard at it all morning, climbing up ladders and steps and chairs, clearing away all the cobwebs with brooms, dusters and brushes. Maisie, the West Highland terrier, and Archie, the Jack Russell, had buckets of water and were meant to be helping, but had ended up having a water fight instead, so they had been sent off to find some bones for lunch.

By one o'clock the gang were all exhausted and flopped down on the grass outside the den to take in the warm spring sunshine. They were covered in dust and splashes of paint and their backs, arms and legs ached from the effort of it all.

Maisie and Archie arrived back with a basket of food: cold meat and sausages, a few bones and other goodies and the pick 'n' mix picnic was well under way when they suddenly heard a very strange noise.

It seemed to be coming from the river. Everyone dropped their food and raced to the riverbank, except Wilf who had to grab one last sausage, just in case. When they peered over the bank, a terrible sight met their eyes – Sydney, one of the young swans, had managed to get himself caught up in what looked like a discarded fishing line, which in turn was tangled up in a tree that carried an overhead power cable. Dilly Duck and her ducklings – Dozy, Ducky, Dizzy and Beak – were busy swimming around the unfortunate Sydney, quacking frantically. A few days before, Dilly had lost two of her other ducklings, Bubble and Squeak, to Frankie Fox and had torn her foot badly trying to fight him off. Her husband Del Drake was still trying to track him down, and as Dilly couldn't walk very well Wilf and the gang had been helping her to look after the remaining ducklings. Beak, the bravest of the brood, was doing his best to peck at the fishing line while the girls swam around quacking hysterically and then dipping their heads in the water and wriggling their bottoms in the air.

'That is *so* helpful,' said Wilf sarcastically.

'Well,' said Maisie, 'at least they have attracted our attention. We must do something quickly. I'll go

and fetch Mr Cowl Pattison, the farmer, and Carl, the cow-hand, they are sure to know what to do.'

Maisie rushed off at high speed while Wilf and the others jumped in the river and carried on trying to free the swan. The trouble was that the mud was so deep that within minutes they were getting stuck. Beak was slowly freeing the fishing line and they decided to wrap it around themselves and pull very hard to free Sydney. However, as they pulled, the tree on the riverbank, old and rotten, gave way, bringing the power line with it. There was a strange sizzling noise as the cable hit the water, which reminded Wilf of Mrs Hard-Up frying sausages for breakfast.

What a mess! Best Friend William, Mutt Next Door Joe, Pretty Polly Poodle, Archie, the Jack Russell, and Wilf were all stuck in the mud at the bottom of the river. Sydney, the young swan, was almost free of the line but feeling very sorry for himself, and Dilly and her ducklings were trying their best to comfort him. What were they going to do?

Suddenly, there was the chugging sound of an engine and Wilf recognised Maisie's frantic barking. It was the farmer, Mr Cowl Pattison, on his tractor, with Carl, the cow-hand, and Mr Hard-Up on their bikes close behind. When Mr Hard-Up spotted Wilf, he was furious.

'Wilf, I've been looking for you for hours!' he

shouted. 'Because of you Mrs Hard-Up and I are going to be late for Melissa's parents evening. And another thing, there is no electricity in the village – if this is something to do with you, you'll be grounded for at least three weeks, no, a month, without a sniff of a bone or a sausage – or anything!'

'Now, come on, Mr Hard-Up,' said Mr Cowl Pattison. 'Calm down, your lad and his mates are in a bit of a pickle, that's for sure, but I'm sure they were only trying to help.'

So, without further ado, the farmer threw a strong rope into the river, and one by one each member of the gang were pulled to safety. Carl, the cow-hand, rescued Sydney, and then Dilly Duck and her brood in a big fishing net, and said he would take them back to the farm, where they could use the pond and be properly looked after, and the vet, Paddy Patchit, could treat Sydney's injuries and Dilly's foot.

Later that night at the farm, wrapped in blankets and drinking steaming cups of hot cocoa with hot dogs, the gang were recovering from their adventure. Mr Hard-Up had calmed down a bit as, although he hadn't got to Melissa's parents evening, Mrs Hard-Up had, and Melissa was doing really well at school so he was happy. Also, the farmer, Mr Cowl Pattison, was delighted that Wilf and his gang had spotted young Sydney in trouble and helped Dilly Duck. He had asked Mr Hard-Up if he would mind if Wilf and his friends did a regular patrol of the fields for him

as he and Carl were often too busy on the farm to check everything. Mr Hard-Up had, of course, agreed, and riding home on his bike that night under the stars, with Wilf trotting along at his side, he felt very happy and proud and full of the joys of spring!

3

WILF AFLOAT

It was July; all the children had broken up for the summer and were looking forward to their holidays, all, that is, except Wilf.

As part of their continuing cost-cutting drive, the Hard-Ups had decided to go on a canal-boat holiday. Felix and Melissa were excited as they had never been on a proper boat before and it would be an adventure. Wilf did not like water in any shape or form and tried to pretend he was ill. The trouble was, he couldn't keep it up for very long as he got hungry and wanted to go for walks. The Hard-Ups were having none of it. They told him it would be fun, that Maisie, Wilf's girlfriend, the West Highland terrier, was coming with them, and that if he did not start behaving he would be left for ten whole days with their new friends, the Well-Loadeds. Although Wilf had to admit that he had grown to like Archie, he couldn't bear the idea of being with those three wild, noisy boys twenty-four hours a day. So, that was it, Wilf was going.

Three days into the holiday and the Hard-Ups were wishing Wilf hadn't come at all. He and Maisie spent each day racing up and down the boat and had fallen overboard, accidentally on purpose, twice!

On the fourth night a weary Mr Hard-Up suggested that they go ashore for a meal. There was a nice pub nearby called The Tipsy Toad, which he wanted to try, and it would be a welcome treat for Mrs Hard-Up, Felix and Melissa. It might even calm Wilf and Maisie down a bit. They sat in the pub garden as it was a warm evening; Felix and Melissa made friends with some other children and Wilf and Maisie, after running around for a while, settled down together for a snooze.

After an hour or so Wilf and Maisie got bored and decided to go exploring. They went up the lane until they came to a high wall with big iron gates. They squeezed through a gap and could see a big house and gardens in the distance. As they got nearer they saw some very strange-looking birds walking around and squawking. Wilf and Maisie were soon having a marvellous time chasing the birds until a voice saying, 'Just what do you think you are doing?' stopped them in their tracks. Wilf looked up into a pair of wonderful brown eyes with long curling lashes framed by a silky mass of blonde hair. She had long legs and a beautiful coat and wore a pink bow in her hair. Wilf was speechless and totally in love.

'Will you please stop chasing the peacocks or you

will get into a lot of trouble with my owners?' the vision continued. She went on to say that her name was Suki, the Afghan Hound, and that her house was called Bedlington Hall. Her owners, Lord and Lady Fitzherbert-Jones, had gone out to dinner with their best friends, the Cuthbert-Browns, leaving her in charge of the grounds and she did not want any trouble.

As Wilf was just standing there panting with his tongue hanging out and unable to speak, Maisie felt that she had to take control and said, rather crossly, that they hadn't meant to upset anyone and would head straight back to the pub where their family were having dinner. However, by this time, Suki had decided that Wilf was quite fun and offered him a delicious marrow bone to chew on. It was getting dark and a furious Maisie decided to leave them to it. Just as she was coming round the house to head back to the gates she heard the sound of breaking glass. She felt a bit scared so quickly jumped into the nearest bush to hide. When she peeped out, she saw two men with bags over their shoulders climbing through a downstairs window into the house. Maisie was sure they were up to no good. She crept up to the window; one of the men was putting some silver in his bag while the other was busy cutting a picture out of its frame.

'Come on, Sid,' said one of the men, 'we've got to be quick, the boss said they wouldn't be out for long.'

'Okay, Gary, keep your hair on,' said the other man. 'I'm going as fast as I can!'

Maisie felt her fur bristling and she started barking as fiercely as she could. The men were startled by the sudden noise and, grabbing what they could, started to run back through the house. Without thinking, Maisie leapt through the open window to give chase and managed to grab one of the men by the ankle. He cried out in pain just as a very smartly-dressed man appeared in the doorway, holding the other man by the scruff of the neck. It was Smithers, Lord and Lady Fitzherbert-Jones' butler, who had come to investigate all the commotion. The man called Sid started trying to kick Maisie to get her off him and, just as she thought she couldn't hold on any longer, she felt a comforting and noisy ball of fur beside her growling and biting Sid's other leg. It was Wilf, come to the rescue having heard Maisie's frantic barking. He couldn't bear to see his beloved, brave Maisie being kicked. Silky Suki, who was much too scared to join in, stayed cowering at the window.

'I say, what on earth is going on here! Smithers, my man, call the police immediately!' Lord Fitzherbert-Jones had just arrived back from his evening out. Wilf and Maisie held on to the unfortunate Sid and Gary until Detective Inspector Stride arrived with his team. He was very pleased with Wilf and Maisie, as he had been trying to catch

the bungling burglars, Sid Snatch and Gary Grab, for some time. They had broken into a lot of big houses in the area and had got away with a huge collection of silver, jewellery and other valuables but now, thanks to the efforts of Wilf and Maisie, they would be put behind bars where they belonged, along with the brains behind the burglaries, their boss, Casey Joint, a well-known villain, who had escaped from prison and been on the run from the police for six months.

Meanwhile, the Hard-Ups were worried sick and had reported Wilf and Maisie missing to the police having searched the area around the pub for two hours. When the police realised that the descriptions of the missing dogs matched their two burglar-catchers, Constable Cribbins was sent to fetch the Hard-Ups in a police car, much to Felix and Melissa's excitement. But Mr and Mrs Hard-Up looked *very* tired, *very* grumpy and *very* angry when they arrived at the hall, because they were sure that whatever trouble Wilf was in this time it was bound to cost them a lot of money. They had already decided that he would be grounded for a month with no bones.

However, when Detective Inspector Stride explained to them that Wilf and Maisie were heroes and had stopped the Hall from being burgled, all was well. A very grateful Lord and Lady Fitzherbert-Jones asked Smithers to serve everyone tea, hot chocolate and biscuits in the Drawing Room and

insisted that the Hard-Ups accept a large reward for Wilf and Maisie's great courage in saving their silver and paintings, as well as their beloved Silky Suki.

Everyone was happy. The Hard-Ups decided to use some of their reward money for an extra week's holiday, which delighted Felix and Melissa. Silky Suki invited Wilf and Maisie to the Hall for a celebration bone and biscuit ball, and introduced them to her boyfriend, Winston, the Irish wolfhound, and the rest of her friends. They were even allowed to chase the peacocks! Wilf, who had had a brush and was wearing a smart red and white spotted bow tie for the occasion, felt very proud of his brave, pretty Maisie who had also had a special brush and was wearing her favourite striped scarf. She told Wilf how silly she had been to be jealous of Silky Suki but how happy she was when he came to her rescue. That night, under the stars, over a lovely juicy marrow bone, they promised each other, paw on paw, to stay friends forever and ever.

4

WILF AND THE HOT-AIR BALLOON

It was a hot, sunny August bank holiday weekend and the village of Montmorency St Peters was in a fever of excitement. Lord and Lady Hetherington-Smythe of Montmorency Hall were hosting the first ever fundraising Summer Fair. They thought that by holding the Fair they would not only raise welcome funds for the upkeep of the Hall but could also give the villagers a treat and make some much needed donations to struggling local organisations and businesses.

Wilf and Maisie were really excited too; their new best friends, Silky Suki of Bedlington Hall and her boy-friend, Winston the wolfhound, were coming to stay at Montmorency Hall with their owners, the Fitzherbert-Jones, and Posh Algie, the English Setter, who lived at the Hall, had promised everyone a sneak preview of the Fair's main attraction, a large red hot-air balloon, and a doggy bag each of prime selected bones, courtesy of Mrs Beatit, the Hall's cook, who adored Algie.

The Hard-Ups had decided to take a picnic and go for the day with Felix and Melissa. Wilf and Maisie were under strict instructions to stay with them at all times and not to wander off. They had to think of a way to sneak off and meet Algie and the others for the Grand Tour.

Saturday dawned bright and sunny. The Hard-Ups arrived at the Hall at 10 am, just in time for the Fair to open. While they were busy talking to their friends, the Well-Loadeds, Wilf and Maisie crept off to meet Algie. Silky Suki, the Afghan Hound, and Winston, the Irish wolfhound, had arrived too, but as Suki had been entered for the Best Dressed Dog and Best of Breed categories in the Montmorency Dog Show at 10.30, they could not come on the tour. Not to be outdone by Silky Suki, Maisie had entered as well, and Wilf and Algie couldn't wait to get away as neither of them wanted to watch the battle of the 'Dog Divas'!

The showground, with its many brightly-coloured stalls and fairground rides, was still quiet as it was early and people were still arriving. Algie took Wilf everywhere ending up at the site of the main attraction, the big red hot-air balloon, safely tethered to its moorings and awaiting the arrival of the Mayor at eleven o'clock for the grand opening and the first flight of the day.

Wilf and Algie clambered up the sides of the wicker basket to see what was inside. Wilf spotted the

AS 781
GB

hamper first and, in spite of Algie's pleas of, 'I say, old chap, I don't think that's a frightfully good idea,' tumbled excitedly head-first into the basket. He couldn't wait to see what goodies were inside! And, oh, what goodies there were – wafer-thin sandwiches, cold ham, beef and chicken, pork pies, succulent sausages, as well as a large fruitcake and several bottles of chilled champagne, ginger beer and lemonade. Cold sausages were Wilf's top favourite and before you could say 'cats and rabbits' he had wolfed down half a dozen. By this time Algie had joined in, but just as they were considering tucking into some rather nice roast beef, they heard a very strange sound. It was coming from underneath a striped rug on the other side of the basket. Wilf and Algie looked at each other; they were not alone!

'That sounds jolly like snoring,' declared Algie. Together, they lifted a corner of the rug. There, fast asleep, was Precious Posy, the Pekinese, who belonged to Miss Pinkerton, the postmistress.

Posy, who was Miss Pinkerton's pride and joy, had also been entered in the Best Dressed Dog category of the Dog Show but, getting bored with being brushed and pulled about, she escaped to explore. She wanted to be a real dog for a change and chill out with friends and maybe even roll in some mud! However, her little adventure soon went wrong when she found the balloon and fell in by mistake while trying to look inside. She was really scared and tried

to climb out but her plump little legs wouldn't let her and no one heard her cries for help. Finally, exhausted, she fell asleep under the rug.

As Wilf and Algie were deciding what to do, Precious Posy woke up and, terrified to find two strange dogs peering over her, leapt up and started trying once again to jump out of the basket. The sudden movement jolted the balloon from its moorings, and a gust of wind lifted the balloon into the air. 'Oh, my word, we're flying, old boy!' cried Algie, but Wilf was too busy peeping over the edge of the basket. The ground was looking further and further away and he could see tiny people running around shouting and pointing up at the sky.

Feeling rather sick, Wilf fell back into the basket to consider what to do next, while Algie was trying his best to calm Precious Posy down. Wilf wished Maisie was there and not in that silly dog show because she always knew what to do. The wind was quite strong now and blowing them perilously close to some farm buildings. Wilf suddenly had a brainwave; he remembered Melissa watching a programme on television with two men in a balloon throwing things out of it. Maybe if they were lighter they would go higher and with a bit of luck not hit anything! Sadly, the hamper would have to go. Precious Posy was whimpering quietly in the corner so Wilf and Algie set to it. Over the side went the cold meat and pork pies, the sandwiches and the

fruitcake. Wilf was just bracing himself to part with the sausages when 'Bang!' There was a flash of light and suddenly the balloon was going down very fast... Everything went black.

When Wilf came round, Algie was standing over him anxiously. 'Are you all right, old chap? We hit a power cable and you've had a nasty bang on the head.'

Wilf was fine, just cross about losing the sausages, especially as they had managed to land. Precious Posy, her pink bow slightly to one side, was pressed against the side of the basket looking very poorly indeed. Wilf and Algie peered out to inspect the damage – they had landed on their side in a big field, which Wilf recognised as farmland belonging to Mr Ponsonby-Finch. A man was coming towards them holding a strange device in front of him which was making a very loud beeping noise. The nearer he got the louder the beeping got. By the time he reached the balloon he was very excited and red in the face.

'Quick,' he said, 'help me move this stupid balloon, there's treasure here!' The man's name was Percy Pick-up and he was using a metal detector to find old coins or anything else that might be valuable. He had permission to use the farmer's land once a month but since the 'credit crunch' he was here every week and he had read in his stars that morning that he was going to 'strike it lucky'! Wilf and Algie were fed up with the 'credit crunch' – didn't anyone talk

about anything else these days? What about important things, like how the economic climate was affecting the quality of marrow bones and how a dog couldn't get a decent sausage any more!

Mr Pick-up helped Wilf and Algie lift poor, shivering Precious Posy out of the basket. They wrapped her in the rug again and moved what was left of the balloon to one side. Then Mr Pick-up started up his machine again and the dogs started digging. Before long they were finding coins of all different shapes and sizes and, after a couple of hours, they had quite a pile. 'This is a real find!' said Mr Pick-up, beaming as he sat down to have his flask of tea. He was just sharing his biscuits with Wilf and Algie when they heard the sound of a police helicopter circling overhead.

Lord and Lady Hetherington-Smythe had reported Algie and Wilf missing, along with the balloon and Precious Posy. Miss Pinkerton, the postmistress, was in a terrible state of shock and after a very strong cup of tea had been taken home to lie down quietly in a darkened room. The Hard-Ups had a horrible feeling that all this trouble was to do with Wilf in some way – this time he would be grounded for six weeks with *no* bones and definitely *no* sausages!

Maisie was in a very bad temper because she had won the rosette for the most Badly Dressed Dog and Silky Suki had won not only the Best Dressed Dog award, but also the trophy for Best of Breed. Maisie

was angry that Wilf had gone off to have an adventure with Algie and Precious Posy while she was in a silly dog show!

An hour later and Wilf and Algie were back at Montmorency Hall having tea and bones. Precious Posy, who didn't want to be a real dog any more, had been reunited with a tearful Miss Pinkerton, and Mr Pick-up was busy telling Mr Ponsonby-Finch about the treasure he had found on his land. The Hard-Ups were relieved that, in spite of wrecking the balloon Wilf had somehow managed to be 'hero of the day' for helping to find the treasure and rescuing Precious Posy. Even Maisie was in a good mood as she had won a prize in the raffle: two pounds of sausages donated by the local butcher, L. Chop and Son. Lord and Lady Hetherington-Smythe were delighted to have Algie home safe and sound and the fundraising Fair had been a great success, even without the balloon!

Later that night, over a delicious supper of sizzling sausages and bashed bones in their riverside den, Wilf, Maisie and the rest of the gang all agreed that the little village of Montmorency St Peters would never forget its first Summer Fair!